Written and illustrated by
Gill Guile

1986 edition published by Derrydale Books,
distributed by Crown Publishers, Inc.

ISBN 0–517–61883–4

Printed in Belgium.

THE MAGIC TRAIN

DERRYDALE BOOKS
New York

The day began like any other day, with Andrew and Jane playing happily with their toys in the nursery. Then Jane accidentally dropped her doll and cracked its head.

Andrew tried to repair the damage with bandages and plasters, but he used so many that the doll's face was completely hidden beneath them!

They did not notice that behind them the nursery toys were coming to life . . .

Andrew and Jane looked at each other in astonishment. All the toys were as big as they were – or perhaps *they* were as small as the toys!

Before they could decide one way or the other, Andrew's teddy bear asked them to climb onto the toy train, along with the injured doll so that they could go to Toyland to see the Toymender. Their journey would be taking them through four very strange lands.

The train blew its whistle and puff-puffed its way out of the nursery and into the Land of Sweets, where everything could be eaten.

The train sped along a chocolate road surrounded by trees made of candy canes, topped with cotton candy. They passed fields of flowers made of a colorful assortment of taffy and gum drops – all with sugared petals and minty leaves.

Teddy slowed the train down as they passed a river of lemonade and Andrew and Jane reached out and scooped handfuls of lemonade to drink. It tasted delicious.

Suddenly the train began to pick up speed. It went faster and faster, making Andrew and Jane cling to the sides of the train. Andrew asked Teddy why the train was going so fast.

Teddy told him that they were in the Land of the Goblins, and that if the goblins caught them they would keep them there forever.

Jane screamed as lots of ugly little men, waving large sticks, ran after the train. Teddy told them not to worry, and he drove even faster, leaving the angry goblins far, far behind.

Eventually they passed over a mountain and into the Land of Upside Down, where everything was upside down.

Andrew and Jane giggled when they saw the cows standing on their heads munching daisies, and birds flying upside down in the sky. Families of rabbits hopped about on their heads and even the trees stood with their roots pointing at the sky. It all made Andrew feel quite dizzy.

Soon they passed through a tunnel and came out into the Land of Birds. It was a fabulous place, full of exotic birds of so many colors and sizes that it was like riding through a rainbow.

Teddy had to slow the train down to a snail's pace so that they didn't bump into the birds as they crowded around the train, whistling and twittering.

After Andrew and Jane had traveled through the Land of Birds, Teddy announced their arrival at Toyland.

The train stopped by a toy fort and they watched as a squad of soldiers marched by.

Jane tried to catch a pair of brightly colored beach balls as they bounced down the road, but they were too fast for her.

There were toys everywhere.

A jack-in-the-box waved at Teddy and told him the Toymender was expecting them.

A short way down the road was a curious little shop. Over the door was a sign that said TOYMENDER OF TOYLAND. Teddy led the way down to the shop.

The Toymender was a kindly old man with white hair and odd little spectacles perched on the end of his nose. He took the injured doll into his work room and in no time at all he had given her a brand-new head. Jane was delighted.

The Toymender was happy to have helped the doll, but before Andrew and Jane left to go home he wanted them to visit the Toyland Hospital.

The hospital was full of toys who were ill. There was a teddy with only one ear, a train with no wheels, a rocking horse with no rockers and, to Andrew and Jane's surprise, a torn and tattered puppet with broken strings, which Jane recognized immediately.

22

The puppet was an old toy which they had broken long ago. Andrew and Jane had put it away at the bottom of their toybox and forgotten all about it.

They were so sorry for neglecting the puppet that the Toymender said he would repair it if they promised to play with it every day so that it would never feel lonely again. They agreed at once.

Soon it was time to leave and they all climbed back on to the train and waved goodbye to the Toymender and all the toys.

The train sped along so quickly that everything became a blur of color and Andrew and Jane began to feel sleepy. Soon they were fast asleep.

When Andrew and Jane woke up they were back in the nursery and the toys were scattered around the floor – just as they had left them.

Andrew began to tidy his toys away, taking care not to damage them. He wondered if it had all been a dream, until he saw Jane staring at her doll, which had a beautiful new head.

Then they noticed their old puppet propped against the toy box. All its torn and tattered clothes had been cleaned and mended and it had a new set of strings. They decided it could not have been a dream after all, and when they ooked at the puppet again – they saw it wink!

28